THE DAD, THE BOY AND THE DONKEY

To Catherine Coe. With thanks
for sharing the load on the Aesop journey!
L.K.

With love to Dawn the Decisive
J.N.

ORCHARD BOOKS
338 Euston Road, London NW1 3BH
Orchard Books Australia
Level 17/207 Kent Street, Sydney, NSW 2000

First published in 2011
First paperback publication in 2012

ISBN 978 1 40830 967 4 (hardback)
ISBN 978 1 40830 975 9 (paperback)

Text © Lou Kuenzler 2011
Illustrations © Jill Newton 2011

The rights of Lou Kuenzler to be identified as the author and
Jill Newton to be identified as the illustrator of this work
has been asserted by them in accordance
with the Copyright, Designs and Patents Act, 1988.

A CIP catalogue record for this book is available
from the British Library.

1 3 5 7 9 10 8 6 4 2 (hardback)
1 3 5 7 9 10 8 6 4 2 (paperback)

Printed in Great Britain

Orchard Books is a division of Hachette Children's Books,
an Hachette UK company.
www.hachette.co.uk

THE DAD, THE BOY
AND THE DONKEY

Written by Lou Kuenzler
Illustrated by Jill Newton

ORCHARD

Old Aesop lived long, long ago
(he was an Ancient Greek, you know).
The many fables that he spun are
always wise and often fun.

It really isn't very funny,
playing tricks on dad or mummy.
Don't play sick if you are not,
or use fake boils and rubber snot!
Do not draw spots across your chest,
just to miss a spelling test!

This AWESOME fable's very firm
about the lesson you should learn.
Read it quick and you will find . . .
It's best to make up your own mind!

A dad and his son Alex, too,
were bad at choosing what to do.
They owned a lovely donkey filly,
but their neighbour thought that silly!

Though Dad and Alex loved the ass,
their neighbour argued, "Move to gas!"

Dad watched the man returning home.

I can't make up my mind alone.
Our neighbour's very rich, my son,
I'm sure he knows what should be done.

And so at five o'clock next morning,
they woke the donkey with no warning.
"Come on, Grey Jenny. Time we were
  gone.
It's market day. We'll sell you on."

The donkey, Jenny, flicked her ears,

I suppose you're after wheels and gears?
A quad bike or a shiny jeep –
a giant truck that won't need sleep!
Go on, then! Buy a big machine,
though I am really much more green!

Whatever Jenny tried to say,
"Hee-haw!" the humans heard her bray.

Dad said to Alex, "Let's not walk.
Old Jen can pull us – she won't balk!
She's good and brave. She won't complain.
So fetch her harness, bit and reins."

Stepping from behind a pillar,
their neighbour shouted from his villa,

Stop right there! Don't be a nit!
Keep that donkey fresh and fit!
No one will buy a sweaty mule —
or ass or donkey — silly fool!
Don't take the cart, you dopey lad!
You'll have to walk . . . and so will Dad.

Though Dad had said the cart should
   come,
he now obeyed his wealthy chum.
He bowed and called out, "Great idea!" –
then followed after Donkey's rear.

She clipped along on four grey hooves . . .
leaving piles of donkey poos!
"This is the life," she thought with glee.
"No big fat humans riding me!"

But as they passed the local shop,
the grocer waved and shouted, "Stop!
Why are you walking, friends?" he cried.
"You've got a donkey, why not ride?"

He fell among some jars of honey –
he really found it VERY funny.
"You ride!" Dad gave his son a poke.
He didn't want to be a joke.

They set off down the road again
while Alex settled back on Jen.
She didn't mind the little lad
who weighed a great deal less than Dad.

But soon they reached a farm beyond,
where a boy sat grinning by the pond.
Alex knew this thug from school –
he was a bully, mean and cruel.

"Poor likkle Al!" the bully scoffed.
"Your muscles are all limp and soft!"

You have to ride the poor old donkey
or your legs get weak and wonky.
You're just a weedy wiggly worm –
that's why your dad can't have a turn.

So Alex begged his dad to ride.

"Oh no!" puffed Jenny. "This is bad!
It's harder work to carry Dad!"

The loyal donkey trotted on –
but next they passed a marathon!
"You lazy oaf!" cried runner one.

"How selfish!' wheezed the next to come.

Why should the dad ride like a king?
His son is walking – poor young thing!

"It's the meanest thing I've ever heard!"
puffed the runner coming third.
They sprinted by and yelled at Dad:

Budge up, Big Guy! Share with your lad!

So what should Dad and Alex do?
Would there be room on Jen for two?
"Come," said Dad. "Climb up and try.
We'll both ride Jen. Pray she won't die!"

The poor grey donkey hung her head . . .
she sagged just like a broken bed.
"Great!" she groaned. "Now Dad *and* son!
Both together weigh a ton!"

But, pretty soon, came more advice
and rude swear words (which are not nice).
An angry shepherd, herding sheep,
swore and shouted:

She shook her crook at son and Dad.

She swore *another* dreadful oath.

She knocked off Alex with a shove,
"Don't crush the beast! Treat her with love!"
Poor Alex tumbled to the ground
and hit it with a crunching sound.

She pushed Dad over Jenny's bum,
"And you too, Mister. Join your son!"
There was nothing Dad could do ...
He landed *SPLAT!* in donkey poo!

The shepherd giggled. So did Jenny.
She laughed so hard she 'spent a penny'!
(Which means, of course, she had a pee.)
As well as poop, Dad sat in wee!

Though smelly, wet and soggy now,
he *still* tried to avoid a row.
"I suppose we were a heavy load,"
Dad sighed, and got up from the road.

"Promise you won't ride again!"
the shepherd ordered both of them.
"That little donkey needs a rest.
You carry *her* now, I suggest!"

"All right," sighed Dad, "if you want.
I'll take her back legs. Alex, the front!"
So awkwardly they lifted Jen
and set off up the road again.

Jenny blushed and groaned with shame:

I wish they'd ride on me again.
I'm built to bear things on my back,
and not be carried like a sack!

All the cows and horses laughed.

"What *are* you doing?" people asked
as Dad and Alex struggled past.

They reached the bridge above the river.
But Jenny's nerves were all aquiver,
She did not want to enter town
while being carried upside down.

She struggled, brayed, fought, bit and
squirmed.
She kicked out hard. She jerked and
turned . . .

till Dad and Alex let her go . . .
She dived into the brook below!

They pleaded, but Jen swam away.
She only turned her head to bray:
"Forget it! I won't stay behind.
Good owners need to know their minds!
I hope before I reach the sea
I'll find someone who values ME!"

With no one weighing down her saddle,
Jen soon was gone, swimming donkey
paddle.

So what could Dad and son do then?
They had no cash from selling Jen.
They couldn't buy a shiny jeep –
no bike nor something really cheap.

Their work was harder than before.
They had no donkey any more.
So each one had to do their part . . .
and learn to pull the donkey cart!

Dad stood between the shafts and said,

My boy, we've been too easily led!
We've let too many others say
that we should run our lives their way.
Because we tried to please the lot,
we lost what we'd already got!

So, Aesop's tale of who should ride
shows all of us we *must* decide.

Know in your mind what you should do,
then stick to it and see it through!
If you try pleasing everyone,
you may end up by pleasing . . . NONE!

AESOP'S AWESOME RHYMES

Written by Lou Kuenzler
Illustrated by Jill Newton

All priced at £4.99

Orchard Books are available from all good bookshops, or can be ordered from our website, www.orchardbooks.co.uk, or telephone 01235 827702, or fax 01235 827703.